Kay Kay's
Alphabet
Safari

Words and Pictures
by Dana Sullivan

One fine day **Kay Kay** was walking around his village of Bungoma.

As he passed the village school, he heard children calling to him.

"Kay Kay, look at our new classroom!"

Kay Kay looked at the nice smooth floors, the new wooden desks, and the bright, white walls.

"Your bright, white walls could use
some pictures," said Kay Kay.

"I will paint pictures on your walls of animals
from **A to Z**."

"Which animals from A to Z?" the children asked.

"I'll have to think about that," said Kay Kay.

Kay Kay liked to walk and think,
  so he headed out into the fields.
  "Good morning, Kay Kay," said a tiny voice.

"Why, hello, friend **Ant**," said Kay Kay.

"I would love to stay and chat, but I'm trying to think of animals from A to Z."

"Kay Kay, come dance with us!" shouted
Baboon, **Crocodile**, and **Dragonfly**.

"I can't dance until I've thought of animals from A to Z."

"Kay Kay, have some tea with us," called out **Elephant**, **Fox**, and **Giraffe**.

"No tea for me. I'm looking for animals from A to Z," answered Kay Kay.

Hippo, **Impala**, and **Jackal** were arguing about who was the best swimmer.

"Kay Kay, please help us solve this argument," called Impala.

"Sorry," Kay Kay called back,
"I'm trying to solve my A to Z problem."

Leopard was watching **Meerkat**
and **Nyala** play a game of jackstones.

"It's nice and cool under our tree," yawned
Leopard. "Come rest with us."

"Thank you, friends," answered Kay Kay,
"but there's no rest for me 'til I find A to Z."

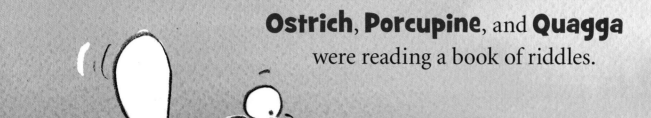

Ostrich, **Porcupine**, and **Quagga** were reading a book of riddles.

"Kay Kay, help us with this riddle!" they shouted.

"Sorry, but I'm working on a riddle of my own," waved Kay Kay.

Rhinoceros, **Snake**, and **Tortoise** were gazing up at the sky.
"Tell us what pictures you see in the clouds," they called.

"I cannot stop," answered Kay Kay, "until I see animals from A to Z."

Upupa Bird, **Vervet**, and **Warthog** were playing tag.
"Kay Kay's 'it,'" shouted Vervet.

"I am already chasing animals from A to Z,"
called Kay Kay.

Kay Kay was almost back to the school.
All of the walking hadn't solved his problem!

Near the gate stood **Xerus Squirrel**, **Yellow Mongoose**, and **Zebra**.

"Kay Kay," they pleaded, "tell us a story."

"Oh, my three friends," wailed Kay Kay, "mine is a sad story about searching all day for things from A to Z.

And I still don't know which animals to paint for the classroom."

Kay Kay turned around.

"JAMBO,

KAY KAY!"

NYALA

PORCUPINE

RHINOCEROS

That afternoon Kay Kay filled the bright, white walls of the classroom with paintings of his friends from **Ant** to **Zebra**.

When he was finished, he walked
along the walls and smiled.

MEERKAT

NYALA

OSTRICH

PORCUPINE

QUAGGA

RHINOCEROS

Until he saw the space between **Jackal** and **Leopard**.

"Oh no!" he cried. "The letter **K** is missing!

HIPPOPOTAMUS

JACKAL

I'd better go on another walk."

LEOPARD

MEERKAT

But the animals and the children yelled,

"Kay Kay, stop!"

"An answer might come if you sit still," they said.

ELEPHANT

FOX

GIRAFFE

TAMUS

And it did.

IMPALA

KAY KAY

LEOP

Say it in Swahili!

Hello	Jambo	Taxi van	Matatu
Good-bye	Kwaheri	Journey	Safari
Please	Tafadhali	Ice cream	Ice cream
Yes	Ndiyo	Cake	Keki
No	Hapana	Bathroom	Msarani/bafu
Thank you	Asante		

How are you? — U hali gani?

What is your name? — Jina lako nani?

I don't want to take a nap. — Sihitaji mnda wa mapumziko.

No more broccoli, thank you. — Nashkuru, nimetosheka broccoli.

No problem. — Hamna tatizo.

My sister is a pain. — Dadangu ni kero.

My brother picks his nose. — Ndugu yangu yuapenda kuchokora pua.

I love bananas. — Nampenda ndizi.

Author's Note

This book is based on the very real Star of Hope near Bungoma, Kenya, home to 35 beautiful children and school to more than 100 village kids who otherwise would never learn to read! When my son, Kyle, was 19, he visited Kenya and became good friends with Leonard Muyelele, the founder of the Star of Hope. My wife and I are now good friends with Leonard as well.

The real-life Kay Kay is a Bungoman taxi driver and talented artist who felt that the bright, white walls of the new classroom needed pictures to help the children learn their alphabet. The children love his paintings and are learning all of their letters from A to Zed (that's how they pronounce "Z" in Kenya).

Star of Hope founder Leonard with Kay Kay.

Ten percent of my profits from this book will go to Star of Hope. You can learn more about the orphanage at www.StarOfHopeCentre.org.

And be sure to watch the children sing their alphabet song!

Asante sana (thank you very much),

Dana Sullivan